The Teacher Who Would Not Retire
Discovers A New Planet

Story by Sheila & Letty Sustrin
Illustrations by Thomas H. Boné III

LAURELVILLE TIMES

RETIRED TEACHER DISCOVERS A NEW PLANET!

Mrs. Belle, a retired teacher, was looking through her telescope and saw something pink shining brightly in the sky. She called the space center in Florida and after checking it out, they congratulated Mrs. Belle on discovering a new planet.

continued on page 2

Blue Marlin Publications

The Teacher Who Would Not Retire
Discovers a new planet

Published by Blue Marlin Publications

Text copyright © 2009 by Sheila & Letty Sustrin

Illustrations copyright © 2009 by Francine Poppo Rich

First printing 2009

Library of Congress Cataloging-in-Publication Data

Sustrin, Sheila.
  The teacher who would not retire discovers a new planet / story by Sheila & Letty Sustrin ; illustrations by Thomas H. Boné III.
      p. cm.
  Summary: While the people of Laurelville watch on television and cheer them on, retired teacher Mrs. Belle, Mr. Rivera, and some friends are sent to Space School to prepare them to travel to Bellerina, a new planet discovered by Mrs. Belle.
  ISBN 978-0-9792918-3-8 (alk. paper)
  [1. Teachers--Fiction. 2. Astronauts--Fiction. 3. Interplanetary voyages--Fiction. 4. Planets--Fiction.] I. Sustrin, Letty. II. Boné, Thomas H., ill. III. Title.

PZ7.S96584Tdx 2009
[E]--dc22

2008055745

Blue Marlin Publications, Ltd.
823 Aberdeen Road, West Bay Shore, NY 11706
www.bluemarlinpubs.com

Printed and bound by Regent Publishing Services Limited in China.
Book design & layout by Jude Rich

It was Reading Day at the Laurelville Town School Library. Mrs. Belle sat in her special rocking chair, wearing new polka dot ballet slippers. But she was holding a newspaper, not a book.

"Boys and Girls, the most wonderful thing has happened." From the front page of the newspaper, she read:

LAURELVILLE TIMES

RETIRED TEACHER DISCOVERS A NEW PLANET!

Mrs. Belle, a retired teacher, was looking through her telescope and saw something pink shining brightly in the sky. She called the space center in Florida and after checking it out, they congratulated Mrs. Belle on discovering a new planet.

continued on page 2

Mr. Rivera, the Principal, came rushing into the room shouting, "Mrs. Belle, Mrs. Belle, come quickly. There is an important telephone call for you. It's the President of the United States!"

Mrs. Belle, Mr. Rivera, and all the children hurried into the office. Mrs. Belle spoke: "Yes, Mr. President...Tomorrow morning at 10:00 a.m...The Laurelville Airport...Bring Mr. Rivera...Magic and Kitty Belle too...Clothing for two weeks...Thank you so much... Goodbye."

Mrs. Belle hugged the children, danced, and said, "Mr. Rivera, start packing! Tomorrow morning you and I are flying to Washington, D.C. to meet the President. He's sending us to Space School, and Magic and Kitty Belle are going to have a special task to do during the space walk."

The next morning, at the airport, Mrs. Belle was dragging a huge box. "Mrs. Belle, what is in that box?" asked Mr. Rivera.

"It's Top Secret. You'll find out later."

The townspeople and the town band were all there to wish them good luck. The Mayor gave a speech and all the children chanted:
Mr. Rivera! Mrs. Belle!
To both of you we say, "Farewell."
We are all so proud of you
and wish that we were going, too!

When they arrived in Washington, Mrs. Belle and Mr. Rivera were taken directly to the White House to meet the President. While Mr. Rivera held Kitty Belle and Magic in his arms, Mrs. Belle insisted on holding her huge box.

The President asked, "Mrs. Belle, what is in that box?"

Once again she answered, "It's Top Secret. You'll find out later."

Then, Mr. President handed Mrs. Belle a pair of red, white, and blue ballet slippers. "This is a special pair for you to wear during your space adventure."

The next morning, Mr. Mayor had a HUGE television put in the school gym. Every night all the families were invited to watch Mrs. Belle and Mr. Rivera at Space School as they prepared to travel to Mrs. Belle's new planet.

For the first week, Mrs. Belle, Mr. Rivera, Kitty Belle, and Magic went through a very hard training period. They had to get in good shape for their trip to outer space. Each night, the children watched as the astronauts in training jumped hurdles, did pushups, ran the 100-yard dash, and even climbed ropes up to the ceiling.

Every time the children saw Mrs. Belle they chanted:

Mrs. Belle, when you're in space,
it is hard to see your face.
But we know that it is you
because we see your ballet shoe.

On Thursday night, when the TV was turned on, the children were very excited to see a giant water tank. Inside it, Mrs. Belle, Mr. Rivera, and the animals were holding onto a metal bar.

Mrs. Belle said, "Boys and girls, stand up, spread out, and put your arms way out at your sides." The children did as they were told.

"Now let's see you jump and float up into the air." All the children kept jumping, but they landed on the floor each time. They couldn't stay up in the air.

Mr. Rivera called out, "We live on the planet Earth. Because there is gravity on Earth, it keeps pulling your body down to the ground. Watch what happens when there is no gravity."

Mrs. Belle shouted, "When I count to three, we'll let go of the bar. ONE! TWO! THREE! WHEEEEE."

As the four of them floated around the tank, the children laughed, clapped, and shouted:
> Mrs. Belle, when you're in space,
> it is hard to see your face.
> But we know that it is you
> because we see your ballet shoe.

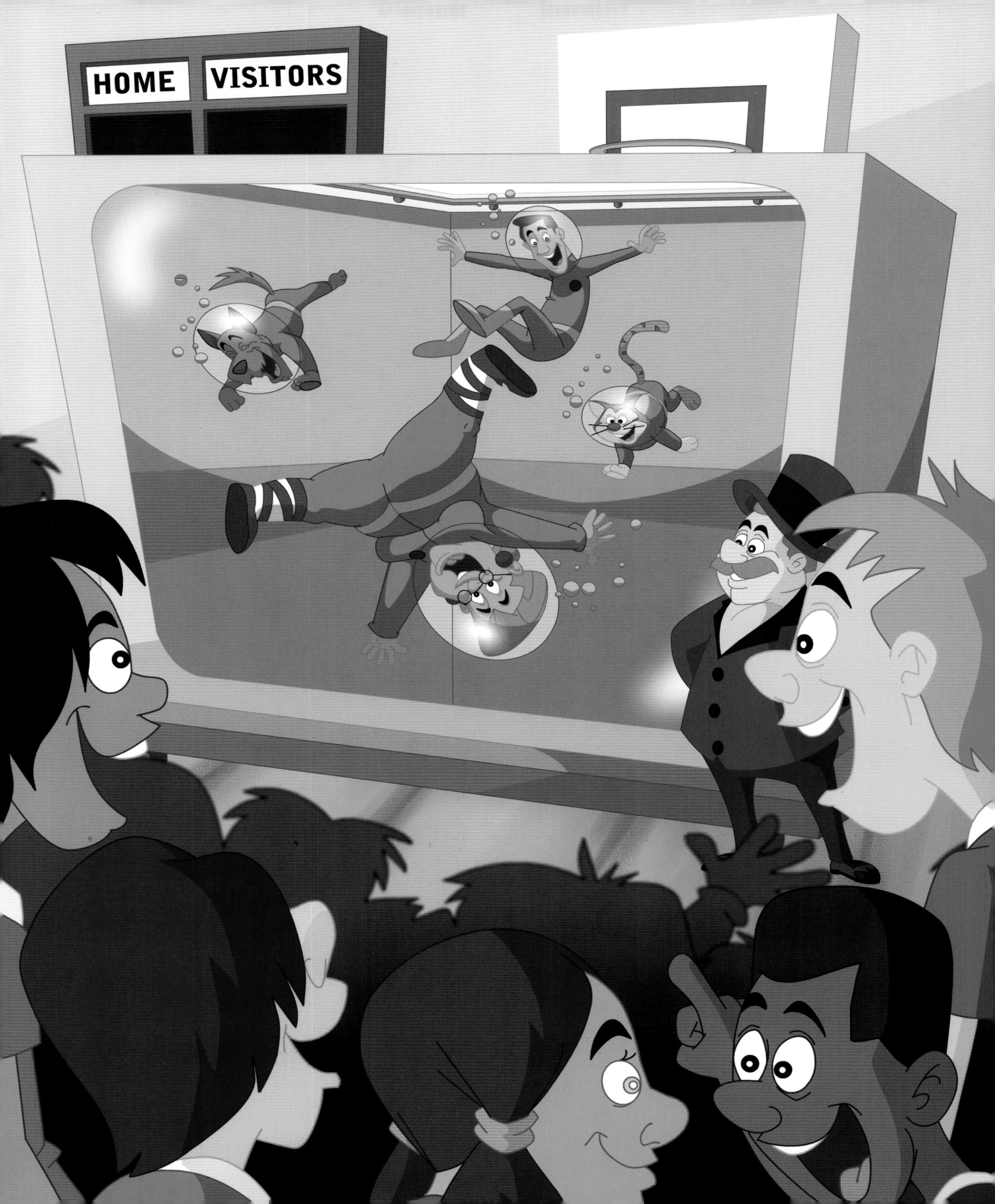
HOME
VISITORS

Finally, the last day of training was here. The Captain of the spacecraft, Astronaut Tom, told his new crew, "Today we will go into a simulated space cabin. We are going to learn to eat in space!"

"What does simulated mean?" asked Mrs. Belle.

Astronaut Tom answered, "That's when something is made to look and feel like it's real. We'll be going into a spacecraft that looks real, but is only for practice."

They all climbed the steps into the simulated space cabin. Astronaut Tom then gave Mrs. Belle and Mr. Rivera lunch boxes and two bowls for Kitty Belle and Magic's food. Astronaut Tom said, "Let's eat."

SIMULATED SPACE CABIN

As Mrs. Belle opened a container, the milk spouted out like white rain drops floating in the sky. Kitty Belle was hopping around, trying to catch the drops of milk.

Meanwhile, Mr. Rivera bent down and put dry dog food in Magic's bowl. The little chunks flew all over the cabin. What was happening?

"Help! Help!" shouted Mrs. Belle. "My popcorn is going wild."

Astronaut Tom laughed. "Now you see that eating in space, where there is no gravity, is not easy. Let me show you what to do."

They all learned the proper way to eat on the spacecraft. All the food had to be eaten from boxes or containers, and they had to drink through straws. This way, nothing would float into the space cabin.

At last, the day arrived for Spacecraft Laurel to begin the long trip to Mrs. Belle's new planet. Everybody wore space suits and boots.
Of course, Mrs. Belle wore her special ballet slippers.

As they disappeared up the steps into the spacecraft, the children were very quiet. They watched as the door closed, and the countdown began.

The spacecraft traveled for many days and nights, and Astronaut Tom showed Mrs. Belle and her friends how to sleep in sleeping bags that were attached to the walls. This way, they wouldn't float to the ceiling.

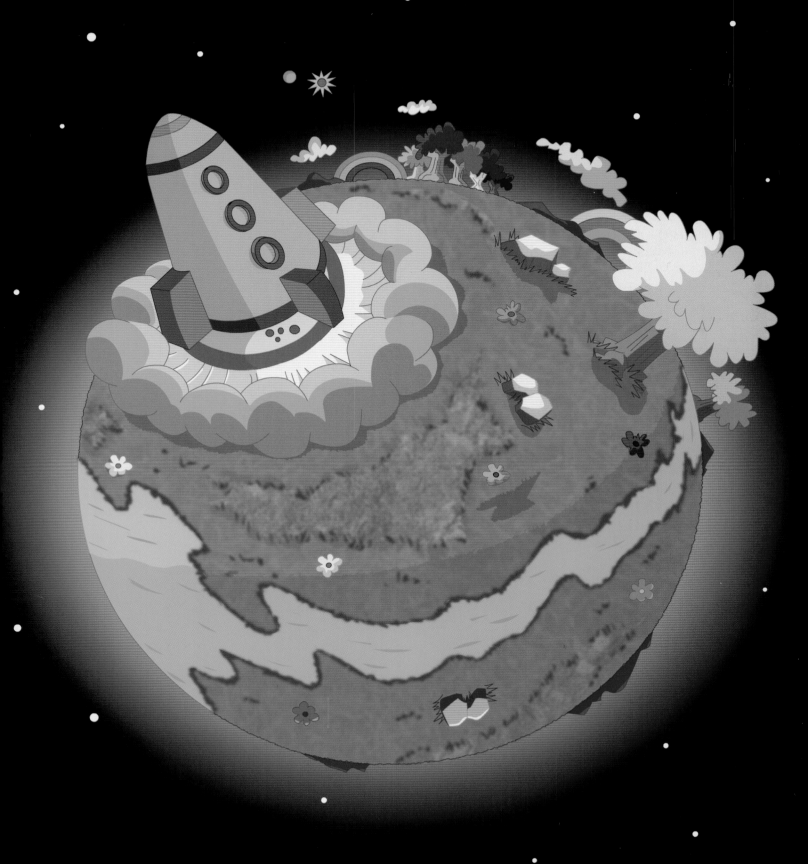

Finally, they reached Mrs. Belle's new pink planet. Up close, it had green grass just like Earth. Everyone in Laurelville was watching. When the Craft set down, everyone cheered.

Astronaut Tom said, "Mrs. Belle, Mr Rivera, Magic, and Kitty Belle, please follow me carefully out onto the surface of the planet. Remember, there's no gravity, so float the way you were taught in Space School. And now Magic and Kitty Belle are ready for their special task. I've practiced this with them many times. Kitty Belle will hold the bucket while Magic fills it up with some rock samples to take back with us. We believe that animals can be very helpful in space."

They filed out in a straight line. Mrs. Belle was bouncing around while trying to hold onto her Top Secret box.

Back in the gym, the children were watching and yelling:

Mrs. Belle, when you're in space,
it is hard to see your face.
But we know that it is you
because we see your ballet shoe.

Mr. Rivera asked again, "Mrs. Belle, WHAT is in that box?"

She replied, "You'll soon find out!"

Astronaut Tom said, "Mrs. Belle, as you know, the United States is so proud that you found a new planet for people all over the world to see." He then put an American flag on the surface of the planet.

Mr. Rivera unrolled a big sign and said to Mrs. Belle:

The USA wants to thank you
because you discovered a planet that's new.
Bellerina is its name.
And that will bring you lots of fame!

Mrs. Belle was so excited she began to dance. She looked like a
kangaroo jumping on a trampoline.

"Now, it's time to go back to the spacecraft," said Astronaut Tom. "We have a long journey home." As he took the heavy bucket from Kitty Belle, he petted both animals and said, "What great rock samples you have collected. I'm so proud of you."

While the others went back to the spacecraft, Mrs. Belle opened her box. The "Top Secret" was about to be revealed!

Meanwhile, back in the school gym, all eyes were watching.
The children cheered and jumped and waved their hands.

One hundred colorful ballet slippers floated all over Planet Bellerina. Then Mrs. Belle joined everyone in the spacecraft. Mrs. Belle was ready to return home. She had so much to tell the children!

So now, when you see a bright pink spot shining in the sky, look at it carefully. If you see colorful ballet slippers twirling and dancing, you'll know that you've found Mrs. Belle's Planet Bellerina.

A Message From a Real Space Camp Survivor

To my fellow space travelers,

Have you ever wondered what it would be like to travel into outer space, to float above the earth, and to walk on the moon? I am not an astronaut, but I came pretty close when I went to Space Camp. In June 2007, I spent a week at the U.S. Space and Rocket Center in Alabama with other math and science teachers. Once there, I learned what it is like to live, work, and play in space.

Some of the things we did were pure fun, like when I was strapped into a harness that simulated walking on the moon's surface. Actually, it was more like bouncing on a trampoline! We also practiced being rescued by a helicopter because sometimes when spaceships land back on earth, they land in the ocean. I had to climb out of the water and into a basket that was lifted to safety. I even experienced a rocket launch when I was shot 140 feet straight up in the air!

My best experiences though, were the ones that I did with my team. The first activity we completed was the creation of a mission patch. All astronauts wear many patches on their space suits. One includes the flag, one has the NASA logo on it, and another patch is designed specifically for their mission. Ours had to include a representation of us as individuals, as well as our purpose as a group. We merged the different ideas into one, and then created the drawing you see on this page. Who knew art played such an important part in space flight?

The highlight of space camp was the simulated shuttle mission. During the first one, I was a member of Mission Control and in charge of communicating with the astronauts on the Space Shuttle. On the second mission, I was the commander of the shuttle, in charge of taking off, flying, and landing safely. Flying the shuttle requires patience and concentration, as well as teamwork. Thanks to my team, we had a perfect mission and were able to land successfully …touchdown!

At camp, we also learned about aerodynamics, which is the study of how air interacts with moving objects. We used water bottles, cardboard, construction paper, clay and glue to create a rocket. After getting it just right, we took them outside, filled the bottles with water, and attached them to the launcher which pumped air into the bottle. When the pressure became too much, like when you fill a balloon as much as possible and then let it go, the rockets soared up into the sky. It is amazing what you can create with simple household items. All you need is a launcher to watch them fly.

In fact, all you need is an imagination to watch your dreams fly! You may not be able to partake in a real shuttle simulation, but you can try making your own mission patch or rocket. Just don't stop reaching for those stars. Someday you may be on a real rocket, and those dreams will become an amazing reality!

See you in space!

Alicia Miller

Alicia Miller
Mathematics Teacher
Samoset Middle School
Lake Ronkonkama, NY

MRS. BELLES CAT

THE NURSE DISGUISE

THE CONSTRUCTION WORKER DISGUISE

THE TRAPEZE ARTIST DISGUISE

NO DISGUISE! THE ORIGINAL MRS. BELLE

THE JAZZ PLAYER DISGUISE